The Final Trim

Every cut has consequences.

The Final Trim
© 2025 Dr. Subin Mathews

Cover design by Dr. Subin Mathews

First Edition

Dedication

For those whose work is seen,
but whose names are not.

This one's for you.

Table of Contents

Preface

This book began not as a murder mystery, but as an idea…
fragile, planted like an aquatic stem just below the surface.

In the world of aquascaping, balance is an illusion carefully
constructed. What looks wild is always measured. What seems
still is always moving. And sometimes, the most beautiful designs
are the most controlled acts of violence.

The Final Trim is about that space, between beauty and betrayal,
silence and precision, loyalty and truth.

I wanted to write a story that felt quiet at first. Controlled. Safe.
But one where, like in a well-lit planted tank, every shift in
chemistry had consequences.

If, after reading this, you never look at a glass box the same way
again, then perhaps the story has done its work.

- Dr. Subin Mathews

Prologue

The mist settled like breath on the glass.

Inside the tank, every leaf was still, Microsorum undulated in the soft current, the moss curled gently along the driftwood like hair resting on a shoulder. From a distance, it looked perfect. Balanced. Timeless.

But the balance was a lie.

The CO_2 bubbles ticked through the diffuser with the precision of a metronome. A green hue shimmered across the Monte Carlo, too vibrant to be natural. The scape had been trimmed yesterday, deliberately. Maybe too deliberately.

A single tool lay near the base of the tank, just out of view. Clean, sharp-edged. Not yet rinsed.

And on the glass, faintly, where someone had leaned…

A print.

Not of a hand. Not of a palm.

Just the arc of a wrist. As if someone had steadied themselves. Or reached in, one last time, to fix what no longer wanted to be fixed.

Outside the tank, the room was dark.

But the water kept moving.

Because it always did, long after the hands that shaped it had let go.

1 - The Death Tank

The Scape Lab, Mumbai | Tuesday | 6:45 AM

The Jungle Room was unusually quiet.

Not the regular, filtered kind of quiet that hung in the air at The Scape Lab, the boutique aquascaping gallery where moss grew in sheets of velvet and driftwood was curated like sculpture, but a stillness that felt wrong.

Nihar pushed open the inner door, balancing a bottle of liquid CO_2 in one hand and a stack of microfibre cloths in the other. The tanks had already ramped up their lights, LEDs casting a crisp glow across carpeting plants and fern walls, but the Jungle Room's main tank looked paused. As though mid-thought.

The 90P sat perfectly arranged, a vision of ordered chaos. Microsorum, Anubias, crypts… all lush. A dense jungle layout, just as Arjun liked it. The misting system had just gone off, and droplets clung to the glass like sweat on cold skin.

Then he saw them.

A pair of worn blue sneakers, half-visible behind the cabinet of the jungle tank. And beside them… **legs**.

Nihar froze.

He rounded the tank slowly, breath catching. And there, slumped on the gallery floor, shoulder against the tank stand, was **Arjun Kale.**

His right arm lay loosely across his lap, fingers still curled around aquascaping scissors. His chin had tilted back slightly. His eyes were open, blank, unblinking. A streak of soil dusted his shirt. One corner of his mouth sagged oddly, as if caught in the middle of a sentence he never finished.

Arjun Kale was dead.

By 11:45, The Scape Lab was closed before it had opened.

The board at the door still read: Opening Hours: 11:30 AM – 7:00 PM (Closed Sundays). But the door was locked, a constable standing outside, waving off confused hobbyists and one courier with a sack of deliveries.

Inside, time had slowed.

Shilpa sat on the steps near the back gallery door, phone still clutched in her palm. Sheetal stood by the reception desk, talking to the police in clipped, monotone sentences. Ravi moved in silent loops, sorting and resorting a tray of tools he'd already counted twice.

Nihar hadn't spoken since the call. He stood like a ghost near the Jungle Room, arms stiff by his side.

Vihaan arrived at 11:53.

Hair damp. Face unreadable. Jacket still half-unzipped. His 7-year-old son had just been dropped at school. His wife had texted him a grocery list. Normal life was still spinning.

This wasn't.

He stepped inside the Jungle Room and stopped when he saw Arjun.

Arjun lay as Nihar had found him. One shoulder against the wooden stand, head tilted sideways. His shirt was wrinkled. His sneakers skewed slightly, as if he'd leaned too far forward and never caught himself.

The tank behind him glowed softly. In it, a single rasbora hovered behind a crypt leaf, undisturbed.

"He had high BP, didn't he?" asked the inspector, flipping through a file Sheetal had emailed.

"Yes," Vihaan replied quietly. "And a complete aversion to doctors."

"No wounds. No water in the lungs. No signs of a fall. Just… gone," the officer said.

"He never sat there. Never on the floor," Vihaan said.

Shilpa walked in slowly, her voice low. "He was supposed to be at home last night. I left at nine-forty. He was editing a video. Said he'd finish and schedule it. That's all."

"Was he drinking?"

"Three coffees, maybe. But normal Arjun. Focused. Joking, even."

"Security footage?"

"Hard drive's intact," Ravi added suddenly. "But the last recording ends at 10:28 PM. Then nothing. Just black."

Vihaan blinked. "That's not a glitch. That's a deletion."

By 12:15, the paramedics had taken the body.

Only the imprint of Arjun's body remained, creased cloth, displaced dust, scissors glinting under gallery lights.

The tank behind him was still perfect.

Soil undisturbed.

Plants breathing.

Layout untouched.

Vihaan stood in the editing suite, where Arjun had last worked. The camera was still mounted on its gimbal. A single SD card slotted into the preview dock.

He pressed play.

Arjun's voice crackled into the empty room.

"If you're building a jungle tank, remember this: it's not chaos. It's precision pretending to be wild."

He adjusted the frame.

Then froze.

A sound.

A faint one, metal on wood, or a door hinge. Arjun turned to look, just off-camera. His brows drew together.

Then the video cut.

In the gallery, the plants swayed gently.
The CO$_2$ diffusers ticked.
And The Scape Lab exhaled.
But the man who made it breathe was gone.

2 - Residue

The morgue at Bhabha Hospital was colder than it needed to be. Not medically cold. Just unpleasantly so.

Vihaan stood with his arms folded, sleeves pulled down past his wrists. His jacket was still in the car. He hadn't thought he'd be here this long.

Arjun's body lay under a grey cotton sheet, one foot slightly visible. The room smelled faintly of alcohol swabs, surgical powder, and something heavier, more permanent.

The medical examiner, a balding man with tortoise-shell glasses and a stack of chewing gum in his coat pocket, stood beside a metal cart, tapping notes into a tablet.

"No external injuries," he said, not looking up. "No trauma. No water in the lungs. No fluid in the stomach. Slight haemorrhaging in the left eye, but that could be postmortem."

Vihaan said nothing.

"He wasn't poisoned," the examiner added. "At least not by anything that shows up in the first round. Toxicology will take time."

"How long?" Vihaan asked.

"Could be three days. Maybe five. Depends on backlog."

"Can you fast-track it?"

The examiner looked at him for the first time. "You family?"

"No. Partner."

The man shrugged. "We'll see what we can do."

He slid the sheet down slightly, revealing Arjun's face. It looked oddly relaxed, considering how he died.

"He had high blood pressure," Vihaan said. "And probably untreated diabetes. But he never admitted it. Said it was just how his body worked."

"Wouldn't be the first," the examiner replied. "Body says otherwise."

Vihaan stepped closer. There was a slight shadow under Arjun's jawline. Not bruising. More like a smudge. He leaned in.

"What's this?" he asked.

"Could be dried residue. Topical oils, maybe? Do you know if he used any herbal stuff? Pain balms?"

"Yes," Vihaan said. "He used an ayurvedic oil every night. Same one for years."

"Do you have the brand?"

"I can get it."

The examiner nodded. "If it was changed recently, even slightly, it might be worth looking into. That patch isn't normal. It's not livor mortis. Looks like dermal absorption, something stuck to the skin just long enough."

Vihaan stepped back.

The man he'd argued with last week over soil formulations now lay dissected under surgical light, reduced to readings and residues. It didn't feel real.

Outside the hospital, the air was hot again. The kind of heat that made concrete sweat.

Vihaan's phone buzzed.

Mira Sen: "You're not picking up. I'm outside The Scape Lab."

He didn't reply.

Instead, he typed a message to himself.

"Ask Sheetal for purchase history: Arjun's pain oil."

Then he opened his call log.

The last call from Arjun: **10:07 PM**. A missed call.

He had never returned it.

3 - The Visitor

Mira Sen stepped out of the rickshaw and onto the sun-warmed tiles outside The Scape Lab.

The gallery's signage was clean, minimal. A brushed steel plate embedded in a beige-orange tiled wall. It didn't scream for attention. It didn't need to. People knew what was inside.

She hadn't been here in years.

The front door was still locked, even though it was past noon. The constable guarding the entrance gave her a look, half bored, half uncertain.

"I'm here for Sheetal Patel," she said.

The constable frowned. "Press?"

"No."

He paused.

"Private investigation. Not official. Family requested."

The man shrugged and buzzed the intercom.

Two minutes later, the door opened a sliver.

Sheetal stood in the frame. Hair tied, shirt pressed, jaw locked.

"You're early," she said.

"I'm always early."

Sheetal didn't smile. Just stepped aside.

Inside, the lab was too quiet again.

The tanks buzzed and shimmered. Lights danced across the substrate. A pair of cherry shrimp drifted across a bed of monte-carlo near the entrance tank, unaware that something had gone very wrong.

Mira moved like someone who knew not to speak just yet. She observed.

The tools were aligned on the central bench.

The front counter was clear, save for a cracked cup of Rotala that had browned overnight.

She caught a reflection of Shilpa pacing across the glass wall of the back office. Phone in hand. Nihar was crouched near the shrimp rack, cleaning the stainless steel lid with unnecessary precision.
Vihaan wasn't in sight.

Sheetal walked beside her, offering nothing.

"I'd like to see his workspace," Mira said quietly.

Sheetal hesitated, then nodded. "Follow me."

Arjun's desk was tucked into a corner office lined with scaping photos and awards. His chair was pulled back slightly, as if he'd just stepped away. Two monitors, one off, one in sleep mode. A boom mic still mounted above the editing rig.

The shelves were cluttered, but deliberately so. Moss cultures in sealed glass jars. Folded towels. Two notebooks with aqua-tape labels.

Mira's eyes scanned the items quickly.

"Was anything taken after he died?" she asked.

"No."

"You're sure?"

Sheetal hesitated. "I haven't done inventory. But it looks untouched."

Mira knelt next to the bottom drawer. It was unlocked.

Inside: cables, receipts, packets of desiccant, and an old cloth pouch with three empty test vials.

"What were these used for?"

Sheetal blinked. "Fertiliser sampling, I think."

"Why are they empty?"

"He probably rinsed them."

Mira set them aside.

On the desk, she noticed a gap in the dust layer. A square, about the size of a medium-sized bottle.

"Was there something here?"

Sheetal glanced at it, and Mira saw it: the smallest twitch of recognition.

"Maybe his herbal oil," she said. "He kept it nearby. Used it before bed."

"Is it still here?"

Sheetal opened the top drawer.

Empty.

"Maybe the police took it," she offered, too quickly.

"Maybe," Mira said.

She stood.

"Where's Vihaan?"

"In the testing room."

"I'll find him."

Sheetal didn't stop her.

The testing room was dim, cooled by an air conditioner and the hum of running water.

Vihaan stood with his hands in a small tank, elbows deep, adjusting the intake pipe on a canister filter. His shirt sleeves were rolled. He didn't look up.

"You must be Mira," he said.

"I am."

"I've seen your work. The school lab fraud case. The antique emerald ring recovered from Thane." He pulled his hands out of the tank, flicked off the pump, and wiped his palms on a towel. "You're not here officially," he added.

"No."

He nodded. "Good."

Mira waited. Let the silence stretch.

"Arjun trusted very few people," she said.

"I know."

"You were one of them?"

"I was the last of them."

Mira took a slow breath. "Something was removed from his desk. Possibly the oil he used nightly. There's a residue on his skin that doesn't match livor mortis."

Vihaan's expression didn't change, but his eyes narrowed slightly.

"I'll get you the brand name," he said. "He never changed it. But maybe someone else did."

Mira studied him for a second longer.

"You saw the CCTV gap?"

"I did."

"And the camera?"

"Memory card's intact. The video cuts mid-frame. No technical glitch. Someone deleted it."

"You're certain?"

"Yes," he said. "But I'm not a video guy. Arjun handled all of that. I just know when something's been tampered with."

Mira walked back through the gallery alone.

The Scape Lab still gleamed, water moving, plants unfurling, filters sighing.

But something in here had shifted. Not just a death.

A removal.

A silence where something used to be.

She pulled out her phone and typed a single note:

"Start with what was missing. Then ask who noticed."

4 - Something Small

Mira didn't call it a meeting.

She said it was just "a few questions," then asked for fifteen minutes of everyone's time. Vihaan had told them to cooperate.

By 1:30 P.M., they had gathered in the central gallery. The Scape Lab was still closed to the public. Outside, a couple of hobbyists loitered by the signage, one of them peeking through the glass.

Inside, the team stood in a loose half-circle.

Shilpa leaned against the reception counter, arms folded. Sheetal stood upright with her hands behind her back. Ravi sat on the long bench near the hardscape rack, his gaze low. Nihar stayed near the shrimp rack, standing as if rooted, arms at his sides.

Vihaan was the last to enter. He didn't speak. Just nodded slightly at Mira, then stood near the gallery door.

Mira glanced around once, then began.

"I know this isn't easy. I'll keep it short."

No one spoke.

"I'm not the police. I've been asked by the family to look into some small details. Not to accuse anyone, not to investigate in the formal sense. Just to understand what happened."

Still, no one spoke.

She pulled a small notepad from her bag. No phone. No recording. Just ink and observation.

"Arjun died between ten-fifteen and ten-forty-five, according to the preliminary findings. The CCTV footage stops at ten-twenty-eight. That wasn't a technical glitch. The file was turned off, not corrupted."

Sheetal blinked but said nothing.

Mira looked at her. "Who locked the gallery that night?"

"I did," Sheetal said.

"Was Arjun alone when you left?"

"Yes."

"What time?"

"Ten."

Mira nodded. She turned to Shilpa.

"You?"

"I left earlier. Around nine-forty. Arjun was at his desk. Editing."

"Was he drinking?"

"Coffee. Third mug, I think. But he was normal. Focused."

Mira made a quick note. Then turned to Vihaan.

"You had a missed call from him?"

"At ten-oh-seven," he said. "I didn't pick up. My son had just fallen asleep."

"You didn't call back?"

"I thought I'd speak in the morning."

Mira nodded again, then moved her attention to Ravi.

"You were here yesterday evening?"

Ravi nodded.

"Did you speak to him?"

"Briefly. Around seven-thirty. About delivery receipts."

"After that?"

"No."

Mira flipped to the next page of her notebook.

"There's a small bottle missing from his desk. Everyone here seems to know about the ayurvedic oil he used on his shoulders. Where is it?"

A pause followed.

Shilpa's eyes shifted. Sheetal's hand clenched tighter around the wrist of her other arm.

"Did the police take it?"

"No," Mira said. "They logged the drawer contents. The bottle wasn't among them."

"It was always there," Nihar said quietly. "He kept it on the left, behind the monitor. I used to tease him about how it stank."

Mira let her eyes move across the group again.

"If anyone moved it after Arjun died, now would be the time to say so."

No one spoke.

"Alright."

She closed the notebook. Not abruptly. Just softly enough to break the silence.

"Thanks."

She turned and walked out of the gallery.

Halfway to the hallway, Sheetal's voice stopped her.

"You think someone took the bottle?"

Mira didn't turn around.

"I think someone thought it was small enough to go unnoticed."

In the testing room, Vihaan poured a sample into a test vial. He watched it swirl, then settle.

He and Arjun had built this place together. Every pipe. Every schedule. Every filter loop. They had sweated over invoices and smiled over ADA shipments arriving early. Arjun had picked the tiles himself. Vihaan had insisted on the steel fixtures. They had once argued for a week over the exact positioning of a single spotlight.

They had never stopped trusting each other.

Vihaan placed the vial on the shelf and looked back through the open doorway.

The plants were still growing. The tanks still flowed.

But someone inside this place had pulled something loose.

And now it was unraveling.

5 - Wrong Boxes

Mira had always liked storerooms.

They didn't try to impress. They didn't lie. Desks could be wiped. Words rehearsed. But storerooms told the truth if you knew where to look.

The Scape Lab's storage room was modest. A single wall-mounted rack. Clean floor. Labels in two languages. All neatly curated, like everything else in the place.

Ravi was inside, sealing a small brown box with a roll of branded tape. The air smelled like packing glue and old paper.

Mira didn't speak right away. She waited until he noticed her.

He straightened, wiped his palms on his pants.

"Need something?"

"Just checking on something small," she said.

Ravi nodded, wordless.

"You're in charge of dispatch?"

"Mostly. I pack and move what Sheetal clears."

"You handle incoming too?"

"I sign for what comes in. Deliveries go to Sheetal or Shilpa. Sometimes Arjun."

Mira glanced at the shelf behind him. Everything was marked. Tools. CO_2 accessories. Hardscape batches. The handwriting was consistent. Efficient. Probably Ravi's.

"There was a package meant for Arjun last week. Small, specific. Do you remember it?"

"No."

"You're sure?"

Ravi hesitated. "Could have been sent to the front desk. If it wasn't logged, I wouldn't know."

"Did you clear anything from his desk after the body was taken?"

"No."

"Did anyone ask you to?"

He didn't answer.

Instead, he reached for a clipboard hanging beside the shelf and passed it to her.

Mira flipped through the log. Courier names. Time stamps. Two boxes marked 'AP'. One for 'SR'. One for 'S Patel'. Nothing for Arjun Kale.

She closed it slowly.

"Thanks."

She turned to leave, but paused.

"What's in the one you're sealing now?"

Ravi tapped the box with a knuckle. "Old lava fragments. Manzanita offcuts. Sheetal said clear it. It's going to storage."

"Mind if I take a look?"

Ravi hesitated again, then stepped aside.

Mira peeled back the edge of the tape and opened the box.

Inside were rough stone pieces, dry moss clumps, and crumpled paper filling the gaps. Nothing remarkable. She was about to close it when something small caught her eye.

A plastic sleeve. Tucked into the bottom corner.

She reached for it. Inside were two unused barcode asset tags. Unattached. Clean. Numbered. The kind used to label high-value aquascaping gear or specialty tools.

She turned them over.

No names. No batch references. Just codes.

"You didn't pack these?"

Ravi shook his head. "If they were from a return kit, they should've been logged."

"Then why are they here?"

He didn't answer.

Mira slipped the tags into her notebook and resealed the box.

"I'll return them if they don't matter," she said. "But they shouldn't be here, right?"

Ravi gave a small, slow nod.

"No. They shouldn't."

Back in the corridor, Mira stopped near the 120P and looked toward the gallery. The lights over the main tanks shifted gently from day mode to afternoon bloom. A few Amano shrimp darted through the leaf litter like nothing had happened.

But something had.

She opened her phone and typed:

"Verify asset tag sequence. Check if AK initials were removed or reassigned."

Then she paused.

Added one more note.

"Sheetal told him to clear it. But she didn't log the contents."

6 - The Last Frame

Arjun Kale was tired, but it was the good kind.

The kind that came after a long day of working with your hands.
Trimming moss. Adjusting CO_2 flow. Fixing that one ridiculously
stubborn piece of driftwood in the 45P that refused to stay where
it belonged.

The Scape Lab was quiet. Not silent. Quiet in the way a jungle is
alive, but low.

He sat at his editing desk, sipping his fourth coffee. The duck-
weed floaters video was almost done. He had shot it unscripted,
as always, speaking like he was talking to a friend, not 380,000
subscribers.

He leaned into the mic and hit record again.

"If your floaters are dying, it's not the light. It's the surface
tension. Break it. Add current. Don't blame the plant."

He smiled to himself, then leaned back.

The studio lights were dimmed now. Only the tanks were
glowing. The 90P behind him hummed gently, CO_2 mist curling
like ghost trails through the Anubias leaves.

He pulled off his shoes and rubbed the back of his shoulder. The ache was back. It always flared when he was tired, especially on the right side.

He reached for the small amber bottle on his desk. The ayurvedic oil had been part of his nightly ritual for years. Smelled like eucalyptus and pepper. Ancient and stubborn.

He applied a few drops to his fingertips, rubbed it in slowly, then wiped his hands on a cloth.

Across the room, a motion sensor light flicked on near the front bench.

He looked up.

Nothing.

Just the infrared scanner misfiring again. It did that sometimes when the room cooled too fast.

He looked back at his screen. Scrubbed through the last take.

The footage was clean. His voice steady. The plants in the shot glowed with that sharp green that made viewers stop scrolling.

He clicked save.

The file rendered.

Ten percent. Twenty.

The computer fans whispered louder.

Thirty. Forty.

A noise behind him.

Arjun paused. Turned slowly.

Nothing.

He stood, stretched, and walked to the Jungle Room.

The misting system had run earlier. The glass was still wet. He reached out and touched the cabinet. Cool.

He glanced at the door. Locked. As it always was after ten.

Just nerves. He hadn't eaten dinner.

He walked back, slower now.

Sat again.

The render had reached eighty-five percent.

His phone buzzed on the desk. A call. He didn't answer. Probably Vihaan. He'd call in the morning.

He reached out to power down the lights...

And froze.

The scent had changed.

Not the oil. Something else.

Something metallic, faint, like old batteries or new wires.

He looked around.

Nothing had moved. Nothing looked wrong.

But the tanks weren't the only things breathing in the room.

Something felt off.

He started to rise.

And then…

Darkness.

7 - Ledger Lines

Sheetal Patel had never believed in panic.

Budgets didn't panic. Logs didn't panic. Numbers were clean, honest, even when people weren't.

She sat alone in the back office, the gallery door shut. A closed laptop sat in front of her, untouched. She had opened and closed it three times in the last hour. The login screen still glowed softly.

Outside, The Scape Lab was as it always was, dim, serene, precise. But Mira had been through the dispatch logs that morning, and Ravi had already told her about the hardscape clearance.

Which meant the envelope was gone.

Sheetal folded her arms and pressed them against her stomach.

She hadn't meant for things to be… buried. Just moved. Discarded quietly. Arjun would have understood. He hated clutter more than anyone. But he would have noticed those tags, those deliveries that came with the wrong initials. That one box Ravi had accepted in a rush and logged under her name, because it was easier that way.

And now Arjun was dead.

She hadn't killed him. She wasn't capable of that. But she had been trying to contain something. The last six months had felt like a slow collapse. Arjun spending more and more on expansion new soil, partnerships, branding deals that weren't even finalised. Vihaan kept quiet, but Sheetal had seen it, seen the weight of too many risks piled on too quickly.

She had asked for caution.

He had accused her of being small-minded.

The last time they'd spoken properly, she had raised concerns about liquidating old stock. He had waved her off, said he'd handle it after the next video. Then he went back to filming, back to being Arjun Kale, the on-camera genius who made everything look effortless.

But she had stayed. Fixed the ledger. Smoothed the discrepancies. Sent Ravi a message to clear the old stock boxes, including that one.

The one with the tags.

She hadn't known what they were for. Not exactly. But they weren't hers.

And they weren't supposed to be found.

Her phone vibrated.

A message from Shilpa.

"Mira's here again. Said she'll need to speak to you later."

Sheetal stared at it.

She stood up slowly, straightened her blouse, and walked into the hallway. Her heels echoed once, then softened on the rubber tiles.

At the far end of the gallery, she saw Mira near the 60P, talking to Vihaan.

Neither of them looked up.

Sheetal kept walking.

Not away.

Just… not toward them either.

She needed a few more hours. Maybe less.

Just enough time to erase one more line.

8 - Ghost Data

Mira preferred systems to people.

People said things like "I forgot" or "It didn't seem important." Systems didn't forget. They didn't rationalise or minimise. They logged, time-stamped, and waited to be found.

She sat at Arjun's desk, the only person in The Scape Lab allowed to touch his editing terminal. The others gave her space now. Whether out of guilt or caution, she didn't care.

His desktop was cluttered, but logically so. Mira had seen far worse.

She found the shipment records folder after three clicks.

Inside were spreadsheets. Auto-saved. No password. One file had been opened the day before he died.

"AssetLog_Master.xlsx"

She opened it. Columns of barcode numbers, item types, initials of the handler, and the last known location.

She scrolled down.

Line 1423.

Barcode: AK-09722-51
Item: "CO_2 Dual Regulator - Stainless"
Logged by: AP
Location: "Studio Desk - Hold"

AP. Arjun Patel. His full name.

That item was logged correctly.

But four lines down:

Line 1427.
Barcode: AK-09725-51
Item: "Custom Scaping Set (Prototype)"
Logged by: SP
Location: "Front Bench"

SP. Sheetal Patel.

Mira blinked.

That item was meant for Arjun. He had signed off the prototype order in an email Mira had already seen.

But it had been logged under Sheetal's initials. And placed away from his desk.

She ran a quick filter.

Eight such entries.

Eight barcodes beginning with **AK**, meant for Arjun, but logged by **SP**, **SR**, or simply with no initials at all.

Sloppy? Maybe. But not random.

She copied the rows to a new sheet and emailed it to herself.

Then she opened the file directory for security footage.

The folder was named "Gallery CCTV – October".

Inside were subfolders. One for each day. Each with video files named in twenty-minute blocks.

October 17: 21:00
October 17: 21:20
October 17: 21:40
October 17: 22:00
October 17: 22:20
October 17: _____

That one was missing.

She right-clicked the folder. Chose "Properties."

Under "Last modified": **October 18, 03:46 AM**.

That was five hours after Arjun died.

Too late for a routine update. Too early for staff to be in.

Only one person had a keycard for off-hours entry that didn't log Arjun's master access. One physical copy, no digital backup.

It was missing from his wallet when he was found.

No one had mentioned that.

Mira sat back.

The footage hadn't corrupted. It hadn't crashed. It had been replaced.

A gap.

A blank.

The absence of a man, folded carefully into the system like he had never existed.

9 – Pressure Points

Nihar was not the kind of man who lied easily.

That's what Mira had decided by the second time she watched him clean a tank that didn't need cleaning. His hands were careful. His silences weren't avoidance, they were something else. Maybe fear. Maybe grief. Maybe both.

She found him at the back of the gallery, crouched next to the 45P, pulling out specks of algae with surgical tweezers.

"You always clean when you're nervous?" she asked.

He looked up, startled, then smiled awkwardly.

"Just… habit," he said. "The tanks don't care what's going on outside. You give them light, flow, and balance, they grow."

Mira nodded, then sat on the bench nearby.

"I used to keep shrimp," she said. "Red cherries. Bad light, soft water. I didn't know what I was doing."

Nihar didn't answer, but his posture softened.

"Arjun taught me more from a five-minute video than most books do in a hundred pages," she said. "You must've learned a lot from him."

"Everything," Nihar said.

"Did you know him well? Outside work?"

Nihar hesitated.

"No. Not really. He didn't talk much about his life. Just the shop. The tanks. Sometimes Vihaan."

Mira tilted her head.

"Did he trust people easily?"

"No. But when he did, it was full."

"Like Vihaan?"

"Yeah."

"And Sheetal?"

Another pause.

"I think so. Once."

Mira didn't press. She let silence do the asking.

After a while, she said, "The night he died… were you still in the building when Sheetal left?"

Nihar shook his head. "No. I leave at seven sharp. Always."

"You found him the next morning?"

"Yeah."

"You remember what the room smelled like?"

He frowned. "What?"

"When you walked in. Did it smell… normal?"

He thought for a long moment.

"There was a smell," he said slowly. "Not the oil. Something different. Like… like when you unplug a light and it sparks. That metallic kind of smell."

"Did you say that to anyone?"

"No. I thought maybe it was a wire burning. But nothing was damaged."

Mira nodded slowly.

"Do you know if Arjun kept anything personal at his desk? Anything he wouldn't want others to move?"

"He hated when people touched his stuff."

"What about that small bottle? The one he used on his shoulder?"

"Kept it behind the monitor, left side."

"Did anyone ever borrow it?"

Nihar looked away.

"Once," he said. "I think Sheetal used it. A few months ago. She had neck pain."

"Did she return it?"

"I think so."

Mira stood.

"Thanks, Nihar. That helps."

He nodded, but didn't stand up.

When she reached the door, he called out.

"Ma'am?"

She turned.

"I didn't touch anything. I swear. I just… found him."

"I know," Mira said quietly.

Then she left.

In the hallway, she took out her phone and opened the CCTV metadata file again.

October 18, 03:46 AM
Overwrite initiated
User ID: Master (physical key)

Only one copy of that card had existed.

It hadn't been found on Arjun's body.

Someone else had it.

Someone still inside.

10 - The Margin Note

Vihaan preferred silence. Not the uncomfortable kind people tried to fill with noise, but real silence. The kind you got inside libraries. Or labs. Or next to a tank that was perfectly tuned.

The gallery was closed for the day. Mira had told him to "rest", a kind suggestion that meant "stay out of my way for a few hours."

So he went to Arjun's bench instead.

Not his desk. His bench. The one near the utility sink in the testing room, where Arjun worked on his DIY builds, prototypes, things that never made it to the channel.

The drawer under the bench hadn't been opened since he died.

Vihaan pulled it open now.

It smelled faintly of iron, oil, and something botanical.

Inside were a few half-used tools, a pipette set, two unopened microscope slides, and a thick, blue notebook. Hand-bound. Pages yellowing at the edges. No label.

Vihaan opened it carefully.

It was Arjun's field book. Not for show. Just diagrams. Light sketches of layouts, CO_2 tests, new diffuser ideas. Scribbles in pencil, arrows pointing to mistakes.

He flipped through the pages slowly, scanning.

Then he stopped.

Near the middle was a crude diagram of a compact soil layer with a note that read:

"Too hot. Burns root hairs. Add buffer or reduce spike."

Below it, in different handwriting, in black pen:

"Check calcium binding on test batch from 23/9. Got that weird tingling again."

Vihaan frowned.

He knew Arjun's handwriting well. This wasn't it.

He flipped back a few pages.

Then forward.

Another marginal note, tucked next to a diagram of a misting schedule:

"Don't use Ravi's batch again. Felt weird on skin."

His eyes narrowed.

Vihaan checked the back of the book. There were six pages dogeared. All dated between mid-September and the first week of October.

Each one had diagrams related to product trials, mostly in-house tools, oils, or ferts. But almost every page had a note written after the original sketches. Different ink. Different slant.

One page simply read:

"Wrong smell."

Vihaan sat down slowly.

Arjun had noticed. Whatever had touched his skin, whatever Mira had found residue of… he had felt it. Worn it. Mentioned it.

But never said it aloud.

Because he didn't suspect anyone.

He thought it was just a bad batch.

A mistake.

Vihaan closed the book.

His stomach turned, not in fear. In anger.

Because Arjun should have said something.

And whoever had written those margin notes had known.

11 - Something You Forgot to Log

The Scape Lab smelled different today.

Not in a way anyone else would notice. The same damp stones. The same aquatic musk of protein skimmers and ADA soil. But Mira had learned that even silence had scent.

Sheetal was sitting behind the front desk when she approached. Head lowered, typing into the sales tracker. Her posture was perfect. Her blouse was pale lavender, not a crease out of place. She looked like someone preparing to be asked questions.

Mira didn't ask.

Not at first.

She placed a folded slip of paper on the desk between them.

Sheetal looked up, then down. Didn't open it.

"Asset logs," Mira said. "Barcodes beginning with AK. All of them tagged to Arjun's equipment. None of them logged by him."

Sheetal didn't speak.

"One of them, a scaping tool prototype, was delivered three days before his death. He signed the order. It was logged under your initials."

Still no reaction.

"Your handwriting is on six of the internal records. Including the manual tag override form. I checked the ink against the shipment log corrections."

Finally, Sheetal lifted her eyes.

"What are you implying?"

Mira didn't blink.

"Nothing yet."

"You think I logged things incorrectly? That's your smoking gun?"

"No. That's the thread. The real evidence is what you didn't log."

Sheetal's jaw moved once. Then stilled.

Mira leaned forward, voice low.

"Arjun's oil bottle was missing. You told me maybe the police took it. They didn't. We've checked every item logged from his desk and bag. It was removed. Sometime between ten-thirty and three-forty-six in the morning.”

“I didn’t take it.”

“But someone did. And someone used the master keycard to overwrite the CCTV folder at three-forty-six. That card wasn’t on Arjun when he was found. It wasn’t in the office. It wasn’t in the vault. Which means someone else had it. Someone with access. And reason.”

Mira waited.

Sheetal didn’t move.

Mira picked up the paper again. Slipped it back into her notebook.

She didn’t want a confession.

She wanted the **pause**.

And she had it.

Sheetal’s stillness wasn’t control.

It was containment.

“You’re protecting someone,” Mira said quietly.

For the first time, something shifted in Sheetal’s expression.

A flicker. A hesitation. A line drawn. Then redrawn.

"I need to check the weekly ledger," she said flatly, standing up. "If you'll excuse me."

Mira let her go.

There was no need to follow her.

She had already seen enough.

12 - The Supplier

The herbal lab didn't look like much.

Just a two-room setup behind a shuttered storefront in Mulund West. Mira had expected something sterile, maybe industrial. What she got was two ceiling fans, three aging machines, and the smell of linseed oil mixed with crushed pepper leaves.

The signboard outside still read "**Kaashi Naturals – Ayurvedic Wellness Solutions**", faded at the corners.

She stepped inside.

A woman in her late fifties stood behind a long wooden counter, arranging dropper bottles on a worn linen tray. Hair in a tight bun, sleeves rolled high. No name tag. Just quiet efficiency.

"Excuse me," Mira said.

The woman looked up. "Yes?"

Mira took a small plastic pouch from her bag and placed it on the counter. Inside was a well-worn amber bottle with a white cap. The label had been peeled away, only a faint rectangle of glue remained.

"I'm looking for the maker."

The woman picked it up. Turned it once in her hand. Smelled the cap.

"Kaashi Formula 7," she said. "Shoulder oil. Menthol, camphor, cinnamon bark. We make a few dozen bottles a month. For private clients mostly."

"This one was purchased for The Scape Lab," Mira said.

The woman nodded. "Yes. We've supplied them for years. Arjun used it. Never changed the ratio."

"Until recently?"

She paused.

Then nodded slowly.

"He requested no changes. Ever. But last month, we got a signed revision form. New base oil. Slightly higher absorption. Less scent."

"Who signed it?"

The woman turned and pulled out a narrow ledger book. Her handwriting was precise. Names, quantities, dates. No loose pages.

She flipped to the last week of September and tapped a line.

"Sheetal Patel. 30ml x 2. Modified blend."

Mira said nothing.

The woman added, "I flagged it when I saw the name. Not because I knew her. Because the new formula included a binding agent we don't usually use."

"Why?"

"Faster absorption. But it can be irritating to sensitive skin. Causes tingling. Inflammation if overused. Not toxic. Not on its own."

"Can you write that down?"

The woman nodded.

Mira looked down at the bottle again.

It wasn't poisoned.

It was altered.

And the only person who would've noticed was Arjun.

Because he wore it.

Every night.

Back in her car, Mira didn't turn on the engine.

She stared out the window at the afternoon traffic, scooters slicing through gaps, an uncle watering his storefront plant, two kids arguing over a packet of chips.

Normal.

She opened her phone and typed:

"Formula altered: 23/9. Signed by Sheetal. Absorption agent added."

Then one more line.

"Not poison. Primer?**"**

Because sometimes, a murder doesn't begin with death.

It begins with **a test**.

13 - Primer

Vihaan had worked in labs that cost more than The Scape Lab's entire annual revenue. Air-locked, temperature-controlled, grant-funded institutions that could measure a change in calcium ions down to a tenth of a millimole.

And yet, here he was.

Running a chemical solubility test with aquarium-grade tools and a kitchen thermometer.

The bottle sat on the stainless steel bench in front of him. Half-empty. Amber glass. Smelled faintly of menthol and something else. Sharper. Almost metallic.

He had diluted a drop of it in deionised water. No visible reaction. Then he tried it in saltwater. Nothing again.

Then he added one drop to a base solution, one Arjun had been testing a month earlier. A mild potassium-based formulation with chelated calcium.

This time, a faint cloud formed. Not smoke. Not foam. Just a thin milky swirl that vanished in seconds.

Vihaan frowned.

He leaned closer and read the label on the potassium base bottle. Arjun's handwriting.

"For test batch only. Do not combine with binder unless buffered."

He checked the date: **Sept 23**.

Same day the oil formula had been changed.

He went back to Arjun's notebook. Page 43. A margin note:

"Check calcium binding. Got that weird tingling again."

He flipped back to Mira's forwarded message:

"Formula altered: 23/9. Signed by Sheetal. Absorption agent added. Not poison. Primer?"

Vihaan closed his eyes.

He wasn't a conspiracy theorist. He hated that word. But this wasn't theoretical.

The oil by itself wasn't harmful.

The base solution wasn't harmful either.

But together?

If someone applied the oil and was later exposed to that solution, through the skin, or even residue on tools, they could trigger a local reaction. If repeated, possibly systemic.

Arjun had been rubbing that oil on his neck for years.

But the new formula?

It absorbed deeper.

Pulled things in.

Bound things.

Vihaan wrote it down, slow and clear:

"Chelation + transdermal agent = delayed reaction."
"Not fatal alone. But with stress + diabetes + hypertension?"

A perfect storm.

And one no one would test for, because it didn't look like poison.

It looked like coincidence.

It looked like a body giving up.

Vihaan stared at the vial. Then at Arjun's old tweezers, still hanging on the wall hook.

He didn't know who had changed the formula.

Not yet.

But he knew this wasn't an accident.

It was designed.

And now it had a name.

14 - Ravi's Breaking Point

Ravi didn't sleep well anymore.

He used to. The kind of sleep where your body knows the day is done, where the weight on your shoulders can wait till morning.

But not this week.

Not since Arjun died.

Not since Sheetal stopped looking him in the eye.

He sat alone in the storeroom, pretending to re-label CO_2 refill forms. The printer hummed softly. The glue roller had gone dry hours ago, but he hadn't replaced it. His hands were moving. His mind wasn't.

He had heard Mira's voice through the gallery glass that morning. Calm. Surgical. Like she already knew. Like she was just waiting for the guilty to say something stupid.

He hadn't.

Not yet.

He hadn't deleted anything. Hadn't poisoned anyone. He just moved a box.

One box.

Sheetal had messaged him late that night, after Arjun had locked up, after the lights were off.

"Clear the offcuts box near the testing room. Don't open it. Just seal and store. Before Mira arrives."

He had done it without asking. Not because he was hiding something.

Because he trusted her.

Because they were a team.

Because when the man who owned half your wife's life dies on the floor of his gallery, you don't ask questions. You protect what's left.

But then Mira had started looking at him. Not accusing. Just… expecting.

And Nihar had barely spoken two words to him.

And Vihaan, Vihaan hadn't even said hello that day. Just nodded. Distant. Distracted.

And now there was a notebook.

Ravi didn't mean to find it.

It had been tucked behind the aquarium test kits. Small. Blue. Bound with elastic.

He only opened it to see if it was old stock.

But inside...

Inside were notes.

Not Arjun's.

Sheetal's.

He recognised her handwriting instantly. Tighter than Arjun's. Neat. Left-slanted.

She had listed testing compounds. Dates. Dosages.

Then a line:

"With primer, uptake increased. Not stable. Needs lower surface exposure."

And beneath it:

"AK noticed tingling. Will switch source next time."

Ravi stared at the page for a long time.

He closed the notebook.

Put it back exactly where he found it.

Then walked out of the storeroom and into the gallery.

Mira was standing near the shrimp rack.

He opened his mouth.

But Sheetal walked in from the office at the same time.

She saw him.

He saw her.

And she gave the smallest, almost invisible shake of her head.

Not angry.

Not scared.

Just… a signal.

Not yet.

Ravi turned away.

Walked back toward the packing station.

His throat was dry.

And in that moment, he realised...

He didn't know who he was protecting anymore.

Her?

Or himself?

15 - The Proof

The last time Mira had walked into the office at The Scape Lab, Sheetal had barely looked up.

This time, she was already standing.

Her arms were folded. Her jaw was set. The ledgers were closed. It was the stance of someone who had prepared for a fight, or a confession.

Mira said nothing at first. She placed a single object on the desk between them.

Arjun's old field notebook.

Sheetal stared at it.

"You left margin notes," Mira said.

Sheetal's face didn't move, but Mira saw the flicker, one blink too long, one breath too slow.

"Your handwriting. On six pages. Confirmed by Vihaan. Confirmed by Ravi, though he doesn't know I know he saw it."

Still no reply.

"You signed the oil modification request on the twenty-third of September. You told Kaashi Naturals to change the absorption rate. You didn't mention it to Arjun. You didn't log the test batch. But you used it. And you knew."

Sheetal's voice, when it came, was low. Measured.

"You're implying I poisoned him."

"No," Mira said. "I'm stating that you introduced a compound with known transdermal volatility, didn't disclose it, then moved the bottle after he died."

"I didn't touch him. I didn't enter after hours."

"No," Mira said again. "But someone did."

She waited.

Sheetal didn't blink.

"You had motive," Mira said. "You believed Arjun was reckless. Expanding too fast. Spending too much. Pushing the company into places it couldn't afford to go. That put you at risk."

"It was my company too."

"I know. That's why you tried to slow him down. You wanted him to feel a little discomfort. Just enough to reconsider. You didn't mean to kill him. You meant to control him."

"You're wrong," Sheetal said quietly.

"But you didn't act alone."

This time, the silence was not calm. It was trembling.

Mira leaned forward.

"You had help moving the bottle. You had help sealing the wrong box. You weren't the one who held the master key. Someone else did."

Still, Sheetal said nothing.

Mira picked up the notebook.

"One of you was afraid. The other was angry. Maybe both. But what you did wasn't murder."

She paused.

"Not yet."

Sheetal sat down, slowly.

And Mira knew she had her.

Not a confession.

Something worse… A decision.

16 - Cracks in the Glass

Ravi hadn't gone home in two nights.

He told Sheetal it was because of the inventory backlog. Told the staff he was overseeing restocks. Told himself he was just tired.

But he couldn't stop thinking about that notebook.

The margin notes in her handwriting.

The word "primer."

The sentence:

"AK noticed tingling. Will switch source next time."

He couldn't unread it.

He sat now at the edge of the gallery, near the CO_2 refill station. The hiss of the regulator was steady, like breathing. Across the room, Shilpa was bagging fish food packets, humming quietly. Nihar was scrubbing lily pipes without being asked.

Everything looked normal.

But it wasn't.

Ravi pulled out his phone. Opened his drafts. There was a message there, half-typed.

To: Mira Sen
Subject: Something I found

I don't know if this matters, but there's a notebook I saw. It wasn't where it should've been. I think…

He hadn't finished the sentence.

He stared at it.

Then hit delete.

Not because he didn't care.

Because Sheetal had stood in the doorway last night and said just five words.

"If I fall, you fall."

And maybe she was right.

He wasn't innocent. He had sealed the box. He had moved the bottle. He hadn't asked what was in it.

And if Mira knew?

He'd be buried under the same avalanche.
So he deleted the draft.

But he didn't empty the trash.

Later that evening, he walked into the filtration room to check on a leaking pipe.

Vihaan was there. Sitting on the floor. Not working.

Just holding Arjun's test tweezers in his hands like they were a relic.

They didn't speak.

Ravi turned the valve. Let the water hiss through. Made himself busy.

Then he said, too quietly:

"You think it was murder?"

Vihaan didn't answer for a long time.

Then he said:

"I think it was designed."

Ravi left the room before he said anything else.

And that night, he slept worse than ever.

Because guilt doesn't feel like fire.

It feels like wet gravel in your chest.

Heavy.

And hard to breathe through.

17 - The Other Key

Mira didn't believe in eureka moments.

Truth, in her experience, arrived in fragments. Never with thunder. Always with paper cuts.

She was back at her hotel room, spread across the desk: Arjun's notebook, the supplier's receipt, the field test vials, and the shipment logs. Her phone buzzed every few minutes. A forensic lab wanted follow-up questions. Vihaan had texted once.

"Tweezers show residue. Same compound."

But that wasn't what kept her up.

It was the master key.

No one had admitted to having it. The logs showed it used at 3:46 AM, the morning Arjun's CCTV footage was overwritten.

Arjun was dead by then.

But someone, someone, had used the card.

And then she remembered something Ravi had said days earlier, almost casually:

"Sheetal approves the clearance list. I just tape and shift."

She pulled out the staff access logs from the day before Arjun died. They were synced to door entries and emergency protocols.

She scanned the names.

AP. SR. SP. RP. VN.

No one had logged in after 11:15 PM.

Then she saw it.

Device ID: MSTR-KY-R1

Entry: BACK DOOR > 03:44 AM
Log: SYSTEM OVERRIDE > ADMIN ACCESS
User: —————
Card ID: **Manual Override (M-Key)**
Acknowledged by: **Secondary Card Backup Enabled: YES**

Mira frowned.

There wasn't supposed to be a secondary card.

Only one physical key had ever been issued. To Arjun. With no digital twin.

She picked up the phone.

Dialed Vihaan.

"Did Arjun ever make a backup of the master card?"

There was a pause.

Then Vihaan said, slowly:

"I told him not to. He said one card was safer."

"Could someone have cloned it?"

"No. It's not NFC. It's magnetic. The reader's too old."

"Then who had access?"

Another pause.

Then Vihaan exhaled.

"There's only one person he ever trusted enough to test the system with."

Mira waited.

Vihaan's voice was quiet.

"His ex-wife."

18 - She Never Left

The address was old.

Pulled from a tax record Vihaan had helped dig up. The name wasn't Arjun Kale's. It was **Rhea S. Kale**, with the S scribbled into the form like an afterthought.

The flat was on the second floor of a building that had seen better decades. No doorbell. Just a metal latch and a red nameplate where the paint had flaked off the vowels.

Mira knocked.

No answer.

She knocked again.

A shuffle inside. A pause. Then the door opened.

Rhea Kale was taller than Mira expected. Slim. Grey streaks in her tied-back hair. No makeup. A shawl draped over a sleeveless top. Her eyes were the kind that had seen many winters and stopped waiting for spring.

"Yes?"

"Rhea Kale?"

A nod. Wary.

"My name is Mira Sen. I'm helping investigate Arjun Kale's death."

Rhea didn't flinch.

She stepped back. Left the door open. Said nothing.

Inside, the flat was bare. Sparse furniture. A single money plant curling up a dead tube-light. But clean. Lived in. Like she never planned to host, but had never quite left either.

Mira didn't sit.

"I need to ask where you were the night of October seventeenth."

Rhea raised an eyebrow. "You think I killed him?"

"I think you had the only other copy of the master access key to The Scape Lab."

A pause.

Then Rhea smiled. It wasn't a pleasant one.

"I didn't clone the card. Arjun gave it to me."

Mira blinked. "When?"

"Fourteen years ago. When we separated. He told everyone I left. I did. But I never left him. Not really."

Mira waited.

"I came back two months ago," Rhea said. "I didn't move in. But I was around. I needed money. He was… reluctant. But he gave it. Quietly."

"Did you see him often?"

"More than anyone knew."

"Did you enter the lab after he died?"

Another pause.

Rhea's fingers tightened around her shawl.

"I went in at three-forty that morning. Yes."

"Why?"

"I wanted the SD card."

Mira stilled.

"Why?"

"Because I knew something was wrong. And I also knew they'd try to blame me. So I took it."

"Where is it now?"

"I don't have it."

"Who does?"

Rhea looked Mira in the eye.

And said, "Someone who knew exactly what was on it."

19 - The Last Seconds

Rhea hadn't lied.

The SD card was exactly where she said it would be inside a small packet of activated carbon, buried in a filter cartridge from a tank no one had used in months.

Mira extracted it in silence.

No drama. No threats.

Just a quiet, loaded exchange.

"He didn't know I was watching that night," Rhea had said. "He thought he was alone."

Mira sat alone in the editing room at The Scape Lab.

The lights were off.

The tanks glowed softly behind her. CO_2 diffusers ticked like a slow, measured clock. She slotted the card into the reader.

A single file.
10-17_EDIT_3.mp4

She pressed play.

Arjun sat at his desk.

Same position as the previous clip. Coffee beside him. No shoes.
Talking into the mic.

"Red root floaters, if they start melting, stop increasing light.
That's your first mistake. It's usually CO_2 saturation, or surface
film…"

He adjusted the frame.

Then paused. Looked to his left. Off-screen.

"…Hello?"

Silence.

"Vihaan?"

He stood up, half out of frame.

Walked a few steps toward the Jungle Room. The sound of
misting kicked in.
He leaned over. Looked at something on the floor.

Then turned back toward the desk.

"Don't do that, okay? Not funny."
Still silence.

He sat again.

"Sorry. Thought someone was here."

He resumed recording.

"So when you're trying to create a wild layout, a jungle, overgrown, what feels like chaos, it's actually about discipline. Layering. Foreground, middle, shadow breaks…"

Another sound.

Softer this time.

Metal on tile. Like a small object falling behind him.

Arjun paused again. Turned.

"Who is that?"

Then, he stood again.

His eyes moved to something directly behind the tank.

Off-camera.

"Wait! hey, what are you…"

The footage glitched.

A blur across the screen.

Not a cut. Not a digital error.

Something moved in front of the lens.

Then Arjun stumbled sideways, one hand on the tank. His expression wasn't pain.

It was **surprise**.

Then the feed cut to black.

Mira exhaled.

She rewound. Slowed it down.

Frame by frame.

The blur passed the camera, only for a quarter-second.

Not a face.

But a shape.

A shoulder. A gloved hand. Holding something small and round.

She captured the still.

Then opened the gallery.

Scanned the tools. The packing station. The bench.

She didn't know what it was yet.

But she knew someone had been in the room.

And Arjun **knew them**.

20 - The Thing She Never Said

Shilpa didn't like silence anymore.

Not because it was uncomfortable, but because, since Arjun's death, it made her hear **everything else** too clearly.

The whirr of the skimmer. The barely audible fan behind the UV steriliser. The constant, rhythmic drip of the RO top-off system. All of it reminded her he wasn't here to say, "Can you hear that? That's off by half a decibel."

She sat alone near the gallery stairs, holding her phone. Not scrolling. Just staring at the black screen.

She had filmed that last video.

Well, not all of it.

Just the daylight segment. Arjun had insisted on finishing the night scenes solo.

"Don't need you staying late," he'd said. "I'm just showing root trimming and a dosing tip. Easy edit."

She had laughed and left at 9:40, just like she told Mira.

But she hadn't mentioned one thing.

Because it had felt small at the time.

Nothing.

Except now, it didn't.

The memory played again in her head, clear and colourless:

She had been packing her tripod near the entrance when **someone came in**.

Not through the gallery.

Through the **side hallway**.

Just a shadow. No hello. Just moving quickly past the testing room.

She hadn't seen the face.

But she had seen something else.

Gloves.

Light grey nitrile gloves.

The kind Arjun used when handling ferts or trimming with new tools. But he wasn't wearing them that day. She remembered. His fingers had tape from a scaping cut.

This person?

The gloves were clean. New. **Too new**.

And the gait… fast. Intentional. No hesitation.

She had told herself it was Nihar. Or Ravi. Or even Vihaan stopping by.

But now?

Now she wasn't sure anymore.

She stood, walked into the editing room, and looked at the still Mira had printed from the SD card.

The blur.

The outline.

That same **glove**.

Her stomach turned.

Not from fear. From certainty.

21 - Bubble Theory

The still image was grainy.

But the outline was distinct.

Round. Palm-sized. Reflective on one side. Ribbed nozzle at the tip.

Vihaan stared at it for a long time.

Then pointed to the screen.

"That's not a bottle cap," he said.

Mira raised an eyebrow.

"It's not smooth enough. Too ridged. And the body's curved. Like… like a gas chamber."

Mira leaned in.

"You think it's a tool?"

"Not a standard one. But we've modified enough CO_2 parts here to know this could be anything. Bubble counter. Check valve. Even a dosing spike."

They were sitting in Vihaan's test lab, a tray of dismantled fert tools spread out across the bench.

He reached into a drawer and pulled out a **CO_2 bubble counter**. One of the smaller, metal types with a top-fill port and a twist-lock nozzle.

"This one here," he said, unscrewing the top. "This would hold around 10–15ml of liquid. Enough to inject something into a water column. Or through mist. Or… skin."

Mira stared.

"You're saying that object… could it have held the primer?"

Vihaan shook his head. "The primer wasn't toxic. Not on its own. But if something else… say, a binder or a denatured trace… was added and aerosolised, or micro-dosed…"

He didn't finish the sentence.

Mira did.

"It could deliver just enough to trigger a reaction."

"In someone already primed, yes."

Mira sat back.

"And who would know how to make that?"

Vihaan didn't answer.

He didn't need to.

They both knew.

Sheetal handled inventory. Ravi handled packing. Shilpa filmed and edited.

But only **one person in the entire lab** had ever prototyped delivery systems.

Only one had the expertise to adjust dispersion.

And only one had quietly stopped working with Arjun four months ago, **without ever explaining why**.

Vihaan exhaled.

"My wife."

22 - The Quiet One

They never noticed.

That was the part that amazed them most.

Not the technique. Not the timing. The fact that everyone walked around, for weeks, blind to what had happened right in front of them.

Arjun Kale hadn't just died.

He had been erased.

One degree at a time.

It had started as an accident. A moment of impulse. A test. But when the reaction happened, when he started rubbing his shoulder and wincing, when he looked at that bottle like it had betrayed him, it became real.

Too real to undo.

Too dangerous to confess.

So the killer had cleaned.

Logged the box under Sheetal's name. Let Ravi move it. Stayed silent when Mira came asking questions. Hid the SD card before even they knew what they would do with it.

Because that's what made the difference.

Not rage. Not hatred.

Precision.

Every step they took afterward was just another form of trimming.

Like an aquascape, chaotic to the untrained eye, but underneath it, all lines and light.

Arjun had grown too big. Too loud. Too fast.

And in doing so, he had left no room for those who built the roots beneath him.

He had stopped listening.

He had stopped seeing.

He had made them invisible.

But now?
They were everywhere.

Watching.

Waiting.

Because they knew Mira was close.

But they also knew something Mira didn't.

She was wrong about the motive.

And when she figured it out, it would be too late.

Because Arjun's death wasn't about stopping the business.

It was about **saving someone else**.

Someone Mira hadn't even questioned yet.

23 - What He Threatened

Mira sat in the gallery's back office, surrounded by silence too thick to ignore. Arjun's notes. The still image from the SD card. The lab reports. Everything pointed to a deliberate action, but the motive still didn't sit right.

No secret son.

No family feud.

Just a man who had made too many people invisible.

She flipped again through the R&D archive Vihaan had given her access to, product development logs, submission forms, early prototypes.

Then she saw the name.

Ira N. Sen.

She frowned.

The signature appeared on three early test sheets for a CO_2 dispersion capsule, the same shape, structure, and size as the one in the blurred image from Arjun's final footage.

The design was clean. Efficient. Ahead of its time.

The name on the final version?

A.K.

She walked into the testing room where Vihaan was adjusting a timer relay. He looked up as she entered.

"Ira Sen," she said. "That's your wife?"

He nodded slowly.

"She kept her maiden name. Didn't want anyone to think I got her into the business. She earned her place here."

Mira held up the folder.

"She designed the capsule?"

"All of it," Vihaan said. "Every curve, every taper, even the buffer chamber. It was hers."

"She left the company after the fallout with Arjun."

Vihaan exhaled.

"He took the design. Said it needed refinement. Called it inefficient. Then filed the final product for the next launch under his name."

"And she let him?"

"She walked away."

Mira paused.

"But that wasn't the end of it."

Vihaan said nothing.

Back at her desk, Mira pulled out Arjun's handwritten R&D timeline. One column listed test results. Another had a rough video content schedule, meant for the YouTube channel.

One entry read:

"Q4 Launch: Capsule Diffuser > Include in docu-series. Founding vision → A.K."

There was no mention of Ira.

No footnote.

Just a man rewriting history before it happened.

And now Arjun Kale was dead.

Not from poison. Not from a random reaction.

From the slow, intentional build-up of residue. Of pride. Of someone he'd underestimated one too many times.

Not because she wanted revenge.

Because she couldn't let him take what was hers. Not again.

24 - Signature

The light in the testing room was dim.

Only the glow from the 90P filtered through the hallway, casting ripple shadows across the floor. The air was heavy, not with heat, but with something else. Finality.

Mira stepped inside.

Vihaan was seated at the corner desk, not working, just staring at the CO_2 prototype chamber she'd returned.

"She's waiting," he said without turning. "By the utility sink."

Ira Sen stood where Mira expected her hands inside a stainless-steel basin, rinsing tweezers that didn't need rinsing. Her sleeves were rolled. Her posture perfect.

Mira stepped up and placed the prototype tool gently on the counter between them.

"I recognise the design," Mira said. "From the R&D log. Early February tests. Hand-lathed. Buffer chamber built for precision micro-dosing. Elegant."

Ira didn't look up.

"Your signature was on the original files," Mira continued. "And then it wasn't. The release version, the one Arjun was preparing to launch, only had his name."

Ira shut off the tap.

"He said the market wouldn't understand the original design. That he was streamlining it."

"You mean rebranding it."

Ira dried her hands with mechanical calm.

"It wasn't just the design. It was the narrative. The origin story. He was going to talk about inspiration and breakthrough and innovation. He'd say it came to him after three months of failure, like he hadn't pulled my prototype out of cold storage and copied it line by line."

"You built it," Mira said. "He renamed it."

Ira nodded.

"I built five tools in that lab. Three were shelved. Two were renamed. I let it go. Every time. Because I thought the work mattered more than the credit."

"But this time?"
Ira looked up.

"He was going to make me disappear. From my own work. From the story. Forever. So I decided to make a signature he couldn't edit."

Mira stayed still.

"You didn't mean to kill him."

"No," Ira said. "But I didn't stop it either."

"You deleted the footage."

"I couldn't bear to watch it. Not after I saw his face. He was scared. And I hated that I had made him scared."

"You used a delivery tool. You altered the oil formula. You introduced transdermal uptake."

Ira nodded.

"I knew the interaction might be unpredictable. But I thought… he'd notice. He always noticed."

Mira was quiet.

"You'll be charged."

"I know."

"You'll likely lose everything."

Ira took a deep breath.

"I already did."

Mira walked out slowly.

Vihaan was still seated at the desk.

"She didn't do it for you," Mira said softly.

"I know," he replied.

"But you knew."

He nodded once. "I didn't stop it."

Mira said nothing.

There was nothing left to say.

Epilogue

Two weeks later, The Scape Lab reopened.

No fanfare. No relaunch video. Just the quiet hum of filters, the shimmer of light over Monte Carlo carpets, and the slow breath of water moving through glass.

Mira didn't stay for the reopening.

She stood across the street that morning, holding a takeaway cup of black tea, watching from behind tinted sunglasses as a young couple peeked through the door. A new signboard had been added under the old logo:

"In memory of those who shaped what cannot be seen."

Inside, Shilpa straightened the gallery counter.

Nihar calibrated CO_2.

Ravi unpacked a new shipment of ADA tools.

Sheetal wasn't there.

Neither was Vihaan.

And Ira?

Arraigned.

Pending trial.

Still silent.

That evening, Mira returned to her hotel room and opened her laptop.

A video had gone live that morning, one last upload from Arjun Kale's YouTube channel.

Scheduled. Automated.

In the frame, Arjun stood in front of a half-finished tank. The light hadn't been adjusted yet. The carpeting wasn't done. He wore a faded t-shirt and a crooked smile.

"I used to think aquascaping was about control," he said. "About making something wild look tame. But it's not. It's about reading what's already there, and knowing when to stop trimming."
"Sometimes, the most powerful thing you can do… is let something grow the way it wants to."

He reached into the tank.

The video froze on his hand, submerged, still, halfway to adjustment.

Then faded to black.

Mira closed her laptop.

She didn't smile.

But she did whisper something, just once, to no one.

"That was your best line."

THE END

Author Bio

Dr. Subin Mathews writes stories about quiet betrayals, invisible systems, and the damage done by control. He approaches fiction like design… precise, deliberate, and structured to withstand tension.

His novels explore how silence conceals motive, how perfection invites obsession, and how people unravel not in chaos, but in order. The Perfect Line is his second thriller.

He lives in India, where he writes, invents, and quietly observes what others overlook.